WINGS IN THE WATER
The Story of a Manta Ray

SMITHSONIAN OCEANIC COLLECTION

For Bill Acker— in appreciation of the profound respect he has for the manta rays of Yap Island, and for his generosity in sharing his firsthand knowledge of them. — H.I.M.

For Kathy Ann, with all my love. — S.J. P.

Book layout: Diane Hinze Kanzler

First Edition 1998
10 9 8 7 6 5 4 3 2 1
Printed in Singapore

Acknowledgments:
   Soundprints wishes to thank Dr. Victor Springer of the Department of Vertebrate Zoology at the Smithsonian Institution's National Museum of Natural History for his curatorial review.
   Steven James Petruccio would like to thank the following people: Diane Hinze Kanzler for her creative vision and invaluable research assistance, Peg Siebert and Blodgett Memorial Library for providing reference sources, and his family for their support.

WINGS IN THE WATER
The Story of a Manta Ray

by Hope Irvin Marston   Illustrated by Steven James Petruccio

Soundprints
Where Children Discover...

Twinkling sunbeams dance about the surface of the warm, blue-green waters of the East Philippine Sea. In the lagoon around Yap Island, a manta ray pup is born. She is all rolled up in her wide pectoral fins and is just about the size of a loaf of bread.

Manta Ray is born knowing how to swim and find food. Unfurling her wing-like pectoral fins, she glides toward the shoreline. A forest of mangrove trees has put down its tangle of roots in the water. Here, Manta is safe from reef sharks.

Knowing her baby will be fine on her own, Manta's mother gracefully swims away.

6

Manta Ray's coloring protects her well. If a shark swims above her, the dull black of her top blends in with the dark ocean below. If the shark swims under her, the white of Manta's belly looks like a bright patch of sun on the water.

She spends her time eating, swimming, and growing. As she glides along, water enters her mouth, moves over the folds and arches of her gills, then goes out through her gill slits. The gill folds take the oxygen that Manta needs from the water.

When the tide changes, Manta Ray rolls up her cephalic fins—the two small fins sticking out on either side of her mouth. Now they look like horns, and she can swim faster. She skims out across the lagoon toward the reef to find the clouds of tiny plankton—her favorite type of food—carried up on currents from the deep ocean.

A blacktip reef shark spots Manta and begins to chase her. She wheels and flies back to hide in the mangrove forest.

When the shark disappears, Manta swims back to the reef's edge. There, uncurling her cephalic fins, she dives into the soup of plankton with her mouth wide and her gill openings flared. Now the paddle-shaped cephalic fins reach in front of her head, funneling water, plankton, and tiny sea animals into her mouth and over her gills.

After eating, Manta rolls her fins into horns again, ready
to travel. Two remoras attach themselves to her head with
their suckers, but she pays no attention to these hitchhikers.
Dipping a wing, she passes beneath a school of jacks.

Manta Ray is heading for a spot along the coral reef,
to be cleaned of the parasites on her body.

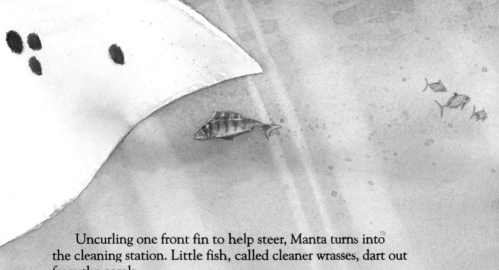

Uncurling one front fin to help steer, Manta turns into the cleaning station. Little fish, called cleaner wrasses, dart out from the corals.

Manta Ray opens her enormous mouth. In swims a wrasse, picking off parasites on the gills inside. Some pilot fish nip at dead skin and seaweed on her back. Others nibble barnacles sticking to the rough skin on her belly.

A mimic blenny swims out of the reef. It looks like a helpful wrasse, but it bites Manta Ray on the tender spot at the base of her whiplike tail. Manta Ray jumps and shoots forward. Zooming off, she just misses getting tangled in a deadly ghost net, forgotten and left to drift by a careless fisherman.

Manta Ray swims over to join some other mantas that live in the lagoon. In an underwater dance, they swim apart, then back toward one another in slow motion. Just before touching, they dip their wings, turn, and glide off again.

Suddenly, they all sweep through the water in a V-shaped formation. Some of the fully-grown mantas' wings are fourteen feet wide. Back and forth they fly like huge, racing shadows.

Manta Ray picks up speed. With a great swooshing noise, she leaps in a high arch out of the water. Droplets spray and sparkle like diamonds. Then, WHAM! Down she comes on her rough, flat belly. The booming splash echoes around the lagoon.

Lifting a wing to pass over a pair of groupers, Manta Ray glides back to the other mantas. Her fin lightly brushes a scuba diver in her path.

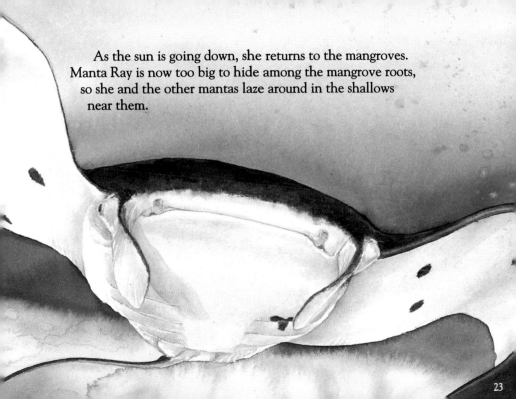

As the sun is going down, she returns to the mangroves. Manta Ray is now too big to hide among the mangrove roots, so she and the other mantas laze around in the shallows near them.

One day during a morning cruise in the deep ocean outside the reef, Manta Ray spies a fishing boat at anchor. It will make a good back-scratcher! Rising up, she curls her wing tips above the surface and skims under the small boat, scraping her back against the bottom.

The fisherman sees Manta's fins sticking out of the water on either side of his boat. They look like the fins of two sharks swimming side by side! He rigs his harpoon and aims.

A bolt swishes close to Manta's side. She starts to swim away, but one of her rolled-up cephalic fins catches on the line to the anchor. Off she flies, towing the boat!

The startled fisherman aims again, shooting into the water. She banks to the left and takes off in another direction, but she is still caught on the line.

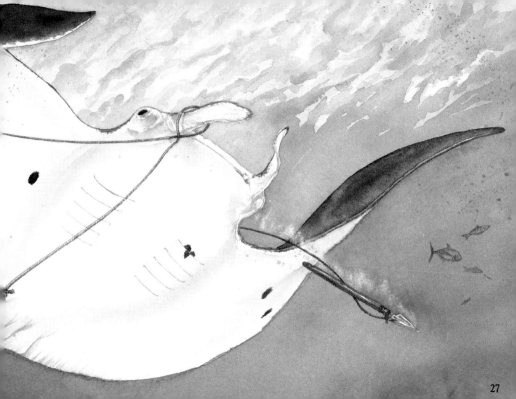

The faster Manta Ray swims, the faster the boat follows behind her. Another harpoon streaks right in front of her. As she jerks back, the anchor line finally comes loose from her cephalic fin. Manta is free! Off she spins, as fast and as far away from the fishing boat as her wings can take her.

Days come and go, and Manta Ray gets bigger. Soon, she will be grown enough to mate. When the male mantas begin to follow her around and around the lagoon, turning underwater cartwheels, she will look like she is leading a long train! Each male will try to catch Manta Ray's attention. When she chooses her mate, she will let him know by curving her wings up to touch him, and they will do a graceful underwater dance together.

But until then, Manta Ray continues to play in the shallows, wing out to the reef, and sometimes leap in the sun above the sparkling, blue-green waters of the lagoon.

About the Manta Ray

The manta ray gets its name from the Spanish word, *manta*, which means mantle or blanket. With its wide, wing-like pectoral fins, it looks like a huge, floating blanket.

Long ago, mantas were called "devil fish." When they roll up their cephalic fins it looks like they have horns. People believed they were evil sea creatures that destroyed boats and devoured people. In truth, they are gentle giants that swim peacefully in shallow waters, especially around Yap Island in Micronesia, the Kona coast in Hawaii, and at Mexico's San Benedicto Island.

Mantas are known for their underwater acrobatics, but much about these graceful creatures— how they breed, give birth, and how long they live—is yet to be discovered. Scientists still aren't sure if their spectacular leaps out of the water are for fun, or so they can smash down on the surface and knock barnacles off their skin.

Glossary

cephalic fins: Small, paddle-shaped fins on either side of the manta's mouth. Also called cephalic lobes.

cleaner wrasse: A small, striped tropical fish that feeds on the parasites it picks off large fish.

harpoon: A barbed spear with a line attached that is thrown, or fired from a special gun, to catch large sea creatures.

lagoon: The body of water between a coral reef and an island.

mangrove trees: Trees that grow along tropical shorelines, with many prop-roots to hold them up.

mimic blenny: A small, aggressive fish that looks like—or mimics—a harmless cleaner wrasse.

parasites: Tiny organisms that live and feed on the manta ray.

pectoral fins: Large, wing-like fins coming out from the chest of the manta.

plankton: Tiny plant and animal life that floats in the sea.

remoras: Tropical fish with sucking disks on their heads that attach themselves to sharks, rays, whales, sea turtles, and even ships.